Arabian Nights

Aladdin and the Magic Lamp

Indrani Vohra

Om Books International

Long ago in Persia, lived a poor boy named Aladdin. He was a naughty boy who was always found creating chaos or playing with his friends. Aladdin's mother could only afford one meal a day, trying her best to fend for both of them, while Aladdin carelessly whiled away his time.

One fine day, while playing with his friends, Aladdin was visited by a big, burly man. He said to him, 'I am your uncle. It has been long since I visited you and your mother so I have come to see you two.'

Aladdin, taken aback, said, 'My mother never told me I had an uncle!' The man replied, 'You must ask her. She will tell you about me.' Aladdin went home and told his mother about the man he had met on the street. His mother said, 'Your father had mentioned his brother once. This man must be him.' The man came visiting again and this time brought gifts for Aladdin. He said to Aladdin's mother, 'I know you have a hard life but I am here to help you. Let me take Aladdin along as I can get him some work.'

Thrilled to hear this, his mother instantly agreed and Aladdin set out on a magical adventure with his uncle.

While travelling across rivers and valleys, they suddenly saw a big rock. Aladdin's uncle stopped in front of it and called out, 'Oh mighty rock, open up and show us what you hold!' The rock parted to reveal an underground chamber. Aladdin was in awe. He thought to himself, 'My uncle is a magician!'

Aladdin's uncle told him 'Go down to the end of this chamber and you will find a room. Once there, search for a lamp and bring it to me.' He then pulled out a ring from his finger and handed it to Aladdin and said, 'Take this protective ring with you.'

Aladdin went down the opening nervously and reached the chamber filled with gems and treasures sparkling in the dim light. He looked around but couldn't find what he was looking for. He decided to fill his pockets with all the treasures and just when he was about to give up, he found lying in the corner, a shiny golden lamp!
Holding the lamp, Aladdin went towards the opening.

He asked the magician to pull him out of the chamber but the magician insisted on being handed the lamp first. Aladdin realized that the magician had tricked him into doing this!

Aladdin was naughty but that also made him clever. He refused to give the lamp unless he was pulled out first. In anger, the magician closed the rock's opening. Poor Aladdin was stuck in the chamber! Disgruntled, he accidently rubbed the lamp he was holding.

All of a sudden, there was a loud thud and smoke began rising from the lamp. A genie emerged from the smoke! 'My master, I am the genie of the lamp and will appear whenever you rub your hands on it. How may I serve you?' the genie asked, introducing himself to Aladdin.

Aladdin was elated. 'Get me out of here,' he requested. 'Your wish is my command,' replied the genie and out came a flying carpet atop which sat both Aladdin and the genie as they flew passed the mountains and the desert sands. Soon they could see the city and its stunning palace on the horizon. Aladdin was home.

Aladdin hugged his mother, as soon as he saw her. He had missed her terribly and realised how much she meant to him. He related his adventures to his mother, telling her about how the man disguised as his uncle was actually a magician and had tricked them. He then told her about the genie while revealing the magic lamp which he had hidden in his clothes from prying eyes.

The whole adventure had left Aladdin tired and hungry. He asked his mother for food. Sadly, there was no food in the house. Once again, Aladdin rubbed the lamp and lo and behold, the genie appeared!

He asked the genie for some food and was presented with a beautifully laid out array of dishes for them to feast on! Aladdin was in the seventh heaven and ate to his heart's content.

Aladdin said to his mother, 'Now dear mother, all our troubles will vanish with this magic lamp and we will finally lead a comfortable life!' He hugged his mother who was moved to tears. Aladdin regretted being a careless, young fellow who had not been concerned about his mother. He promised himself that he would do all he could to make a happy life for them.

The magic lamp had helped him reunite with his mother, bringing all the happiness back. He used the magic lamp when he really needed it and helped out his mother more. From then on, Aladdin and his mother lived a happy and contented life.